Cynthia Erivo?

Who Is
Cynthia Erivo?

by Crystal Hubbard

illustrated by Gregory Copeland

Penguin Workshop

Dedicated to Nichole Jackson and Tyrone Robinson, masters of the art of musicals—CH

PENGUIN WORKSHOP
An imprint of Penguin Random House LLC
1745 Broadway, New York, New York 10019

First published in the United States of America by Penguin Workshop,
an imprint of Penguin Random House LLC, 2024

Visit us online at penguinrandomhouse.com.

Library of Congress Cataloging-in-Publication Data is available.

Printed in the United States of America

ISBN 9780593889046 (paperback)   10 9 8 7 6 5 4 3 2 1 CJKW
ISBN 9780593889053 (library binding)   10 9 8 7 6 5 4 3 2 1 CJKW

Contents

Who Is Cynthia Erivo?

EGOT winners are rare in the entertainment industry. *EGOT* stands for Emmy, Grammy, Oscar, and Tony—the four biggest entertainment awards that can be won in the United States. Elton John, Viola Davis, Jennifer Hudson, and Whoopi Goldberg are four of the nineteen performing artists who have won all four awards. It can take decades in the arts to become an EGOT winner, but in only eight years, Cynthia Erivo has made it three-fourths of the way there.

Emmy Awards honor great television performances and all of the people who make TV possible. Grammy Awards are given for great accomplishments in the recording industry. The film industry gives Oscars to the people voted the best at their part in making a movie, from the actors on the screen to the people who dress them and design the sets. The Tony Award is similar to the Oscar, but it goes to those who are the best in theatrical productions—like plays and musicals—on Broadway in New York City.

From the moment she arrived in the United States, handpicked to perform in her first Broadway musical as the lead character, to her first starring role in a Hollywood blockbuster, Cynthia has proven she is one of the most talented performers in the world. She has won three of the most coveted awards in professional entertainment and twice been nominated for the fourth.

Cynthia is a small woman with a big voice and an even bigger presence. She stands out with her shaved head and bold fashion sense. Unafraid of the hard work it takes to make a dream come true, Cynthia is proving to be one of the world's most original and fastest-rising talents.

CHAPTER 1
Born to Perform

Cynthia Onyedinmanasu Chinasaokwu Erivo was born on January 8, 1987, in Stockwell, South London, in England. Her parents had immigrated to the United Kingdom from Nigeria. Her mother, Edith, was twenty-four years old when they moved.

Edith remembers Cynthia humming around the house when she was only eighteen months old. In a baby book she kept, Edith wrote that she believed Cynthia would become a singer when she grew up because she sang even when she was eating. Edith was a nurse, and by the time Cynthia was two years old, she would copy her mother's actions. In Cynthia's baby book, Edith wrote that she thought Cynthia might become a doctor as well as a singer.

Looking back when she was older, Cynthia realized that her behavior as a child was the first indication that she wanted to be an actress and a singer. She enjoyed acting *like* a medical professional. She never actually wanted to become one.

"My mom would play music in the house all the time," Cynthia said. "It usually was Christian music, but then randomly she'd play Diana Ross and this [Euro-Caribbean] band called Boney M. who did like funk and disco. She loved this Nigerian artist, Sir Shina Peters, and Bette Midler's 'Wind Beneath My Wings.'"

Listening to the car radio on the way to school introduced Cynthia to an even wider variety of music and singers. She listened to the pop rock songs of Mike + The Mechanics, the soul music of Teddy Pendergrass, and the dance pop songs of George Michael. Cynthia credits one of her aunts with introducing her to the mellow, soulful voice of Toni Braxton and the visionary hip-hop of Missy Elliott and TLC.

"So I was hearing everything all the time, and it never left me," Cynthia said. "It sort of came together and made one strange sound that comes from me. I was singing whatever I could sing wherever I could sing it—talent shows, open mic nights."

Cynthia was five years old when she sang "Silent Night" in her school's Christmas play. It was her first public performance. The applause of the audience convinced her that singing was something she was meant to do. Her mother and her two-year-old sister Stephanie clapped loudest. Her father, who had abandoned the family, missed the performance.

"As far as I was concerned, whatever I was doing was making people happy," Cynthia recalled. "By making people happy, it made me feel happy.

So I knew I wanted to continue feeling like that and making other people feel like that."

Singing might have been her first love, but Cynthia still pursued acting. Two of her idols were Barbra Streisand and Diana Ross, singers who also acted. Edith enrolled Cynthia in a youth drama group. Cynthia was eleven years old when she earned a role in a very serious play titled *The Caucasian Chalk Circle*. The play was written by Bertolt Brecht, a famous German playwright known for writing plays with complex messages.

At fifteen years old, Cynthia made her television debut on a British Channel 4 reality show called *Trust Me, I'm a Teenager*. The show had a short life, but that didn't deter Cynthia from her dream of performing. She was also cast as Juliet in a production of *Romeo and Juliet* at the Young Vic, a London theater dedicated to developing the talents of young performers.

Cynthia in *Romeo and Juliet*

Cynthia learned so much about acting in her role as Juliet. "That was the first time I was able to access my emotions and to cry onstage," Cynthia said. "I shocked myself. I didn't know I could access a part of myself that made me feel the way you have to feel before you start crying. It happened and I remember thinking, *gosh, I just did that.*"

CHAPTER 2
Tumultuous Teen Years

Cynthia attended La Retraite Roman Catholic Girls' School in Lambeth, England. She was an eager and involved student and a devout Catholic. Her faith helped drive her to fight through obstacles she encountered as she tried to build a career in entertainment.

One of her most painful disappointments occurred offstage when she was sixteen years old and tried to build a relationship with her father. Cynthia met with her father at a London Underground station. (The London Underground is a subway system.) During that meeting, he told her that he did not want to see her or Stephanie ever again. His rejection was heartbreaking, and Cynthia had to be the one to tell her mother and her sister what her father said. But Cynthia didn't let his rejection break her. Instead, it strengthened her resolve to succeed.

"I don't know that that is a trauma," Cynthia recalled years later. "And if it was, I learned how to deal with that trauma. . . . I think it comes out in the roles I choose and the decisions I make."

Cynthia saw her father again when she was twenty-five years old, when they both attended a family wedding. But at the event, they did not speak to each other beyond an awkward "hello."

Edith had remarried in 1992, when Cynthia was five years old. Samuel Uregbula became Cynthia and Stephanie's stepfather.

After graduating from La Retraite Roman Catholic Girls' School in 2004, Cynthia attended the University of East London. She intended to earn a degree in music psychology. Cynthia wantcd to learn about how music affected people and their emotions and how people use music to communicate.

As much as she enjoyed studying music psychology, twenty-year-old Cynthia couldn't resist the pull to perform. She consulted her director at the Young Vic, the performing arts theater in Lambeth, who urged Cynthia to apply to acting school. The only school Cynthia considered was the Royal Academy of Dramatic Art (RADA), England's most prestigious school for acting and theater. She was accepted, and only then did she tell her mother that she was leaving university to attend RADA.

Rather than being angry or disappointed, Edith was very proud of Cynthia. Cynthia considers herself lucky to have a mother who wanted to make sure she was always dreaming big. Her mother also reminded her that hard work is behind every dream.

With a few acting credits behind her, Cynthia entered RADA with confidence. Perhaps too much confidence. There were only three other Black students in the program. She was frustrated

when most of her teachers encouraged her to develop stereotypical "strong black woman" roles. Everything changed when Cynthia began working with Dee Cannon, an acting coach and mentor.

"She saw that the path I was on was these strong roles when actually I needed to understand that I was allowed to play characters that had vulnerability." Dee meant that Cynthia should consider roles that forced her to show deeper and more raw emotions.

Cynthia graduated from RADA in 2010 with a bachelor's degree in acting. It wasn't long before she got roles in British television shows. She was cast in a comedy called *Chewing Gum* and a drama called *The Tunnel*. A stage role in a play followed, and then she was cast in her first musical role. Her second starring role in a musical was in the first touring production of *Sister Act*, a musical based on a movie starring EGOT winner Whoopi Goldberg, an American actress, talk show host, and comedian.

Sister Act opened at the Manchester Opera House on October 4, 2011. Cynthia portrayed Deloris Van Cartier, a singer who had to disguise herself as a nun named Sister Mary Clarence while hiding from criminals. It was the same role Whoopi Goldberg played in the movie.

Cynthia followed up *Sister Act* with another musical. She played Chenice in *I Can't Sing!*, a musical based on the popular *X Factor* television talent show. Simon Cowell, the creator of *X Factor*, and his business partner Harry Hill had spent over $7 million on the production that opened at the grand London Palladium on March 26, 2014. Cynthia had high expectations for the show. She hoped it would be her breakthrough performance. Cynthia received good reviews for her acting and singing, but it wasn't enough to keep the show from closing six weeks after it opened. Her hopes crumbled, but Cynthia didn't let the show's failure keep her down. Just one year later, she would perform in the role that would change her life and rocket her to stardom.

CHAPTER 3
Purple Reign

London's West End is the theater equivalent to Broadway in New York City. Big, fancy stage productions take place at theaters such as the London Palladium. Smaller shows are staged in off–West End theaters, such as the Menier Chocolate Factory. In 2013, the Menier Chocolate Factory staged a musical production of *The Color Purple*.

The Color Purple musical was based on a book published in 1982 by Alice Walker. The book won the Pulitzer Prize in 1983 and was made into a movie by Steven Spielberg in 1985. Whoopi Goldberg starred in the movie as Celie Harris, the subject of the book and musical. Other beloved actors, like Oprah Winfrey, also played important parts in the film.

Whoopi was nominated for an Oscar for Best Actress for her performance in the film. She lost that Oscar (but won the *O* in EGOT for her work in a 1990 movie called *Ghost*).

In 2005, *The Color Purple* musical debuted on Broadway and ran there for three years. The show earned eleven nominations for the Tony Awards in 2006. The musical's first international production opened on July 15, 2013. Cynthia portrayed Celie Harris. It was the biggest role of her career, and Cynthia performed it brilliantly. She received glowing reviews and was soon cast in other shows.

The Color Purple musical was revived on Broadway in 2015. When a show returns for a run of new performances, it is called a revival. Oprah Winfrey, who portrayed the character of Sofia in the 1985 film, produced the musical version. When it came to casting its Broadway rcvival in New York, Cynthia was the only person Oprah wanted to portray Celie Harris. She had loved how Cynthia played Celie in the off–West End production.

Cynthia eagerly reprised her role as Celie. Jennifer Hudson and Danielle Brooks were also in the cast. Jennifer and Danielle are two powerful singers. Cynthia more than held her own in such a talented cast. She received spectacular reviews. Cynthia, her castmates, and the show earned

Cynthia and Jennifer Hudson

numerous nominations for awards. The most prestigious nominations were for Tony Awards in four categories. Cynthia was nominated for Best Performance by an Actress in a Leading Role in a Musical.

The Color Purple had been nominated in a few of the same categories as *Hamilton*, a huge hit musical that had captivated all of America and earned sixteen Tony nominations.

During the Tony Awards ceremony on June 12, 2016, at the Beacon Theatre on Broadway, the Tony Award for Best Performance by an Actress in a Leading Role in a Musical was awarded to Cynthia Erivo.

A storm of joyous applause thundered throughout the theater when Cynthia was announced the winner. After being presented with the Tony, Cynthia held it up and tearfully said, "Hi, Mummy, look!" Edith, standing in the audience, smiled proudly at her daughter and blew her a kiss. Cynthia thanked Oprah for producing the show and Alice Walker for writing the novel *The Color Purple*.

She ended her acceptance speech by naming cast members who worked most closely with her.

"Danielle, Jennifer Hudson, Heather Headley, Joaquina Kalukango, you are wonderful women and I thank you very much for looking into my eyes every night onstage, for making me a stronger woman onstage . . . thank you, American Theatre Wing, for making a London girl very, very happy!"

The Color Purple was the breakout hit Cynthia had been working toward. She became a highly sought-after actress and singer. She was able to use her voice to support causes she believes in. She sang in a concert on September 12, 2016, to raise money for the Brady Center, an organization that tries to combat gun violence.

The cast of *The Color Purple* had sung on the *Today* show on May 3, 2016. The performance was so good, they were nominated for a Daytime Emmy Award! On April 28, 2017, the cast won the Emmy for Outstanding Musical Performance in a Daytime Program. Cynthia already had the *T* in the elusive EGOT. Now she had the *E*. She had received the *G*, too, on February 12, 2017, when the cast of *The Color Purple* won the Grammy Award for Best Musical Theater Album.

CHAPTER 4
First Films

Cynthia starred in two movies in 2018. *Widows*, the first movie she was ever cast in, was not a musical. It was a drama about a robbery. Steve McQueen, the film's director, offered Cynthia the role of Belle, one of the principal leads, after seeing her performance in *The Color Purple*. The director cast her without an audition based solely on the strength and emotion Cynthia displayed as Celie. Cynthia's second 2018 film, *Bad Times at the El Royale*, was not as highly praised as *Widows*. Cynthia herself received high praise for her acting and the short moments of singing she did in the film.

When director Seith Mann was set to direct a movie about abolitionist Harriet Tubman,

Cynthia was one of the actors whose name had been mentioned as a good fit for the role. At five feet and one inch tall, Cynthia is small, just like Harriet, who led three hundred slaves to freedom. Cynthia is also a fitness fan who loves to work out. Her athletic build was suited for the role of Harriet. Seith wanted to be absolutely sure that Cynthia was the right person to bring Harriet to life on screen. He decided to see her in *The Color Purple*.

Harriet Tubman

"I heard she was incredible, but for a project of this importance, I needed to see it for myself," Seith said. "Before I saw it, a writer of mine told me, 'There is going to be a moment in the play where you're going to find yourself on your feet, you're not going to know how you got there, and you're going to be clapping and crying. And you're going to look to your left and your right, and everybody is going to be doing the same thing.'"

Seith saw the show. At the end, he was crying and applauding with the rest of the audience, just as he had been told. "She just commands that stage," Seith said. "The power she had was the kind of power that Harriet had."

Seith gave the role of Harriet Tubman to Cynthia, and filming began in October 2018. It did not come without controversy. Some Americans were unhappy that a Nigerian British actor had been cast as such a prominent Black

American historical figure. Cynthia understood the criticism and vowed to do her very best to honestly and honorably portray Harriet.

The movie was released on November 1, 2019. Cynthia gave such a good performance, she was nominated for a Golden Globe Award for Best Performance by an Actress in a Motion Picture—Drama. She was also nominated for an Academy Award for Best Actress. Academy

Awards are also called Oscars—the *O* in EGOT. If the acting nomination wasn't enough, Cynthia was also nominated for Music: Best Original Song—for "Stand Up," which she cowrote with Joshuah Campbell and recorded for the movie's soundtrack. Cynthia didn't win the Oscar for either category, but she was thrilled to have been nominated. Twice!

Cynthia became a producer for the first time in 2019. (A producer makes decisions about business and money for movies, television, and theater shows.) Cynthia produced and voiced the lead character of Raylene Watts in a science fiction thriller podcast called *Carrier*. A podcast is an audio show that comes out in a series of episodes that people can listen to.

Cynthia's career kept climbing. She starred in *The Outsider*, a television adaptation of a Stephen King novel, in 2020. In 2021, she had a role in a sci-fi film called *Chaos Walking*, starring Tom

Holland of Spider-Man fame. That project was released on March 5, 2021. The same month, Cynthia returned to television in *Genius: Aretha*. Cynthia played Aretha Franklin, the soul singer who was also one of her lifelong idols.

CHAPTER 5
Making Her Own Music

The fall of 2021 brought one of Cynthia's most personal projects. She released her debut solo album, *Ch.1, Vs. 1* (pronounced Chapter One, Verse One). It was released on September 17. Cynthia wrote her first song when she was sixteen years old. The songs on her album have very personal meanings. The song "You're Not Here" serves as a letter to her father about the pain of growing up without him. "This is me admitting that there are things that he's missed and I'm sad that he's missed them," Cynthia said.

The song "Mama" is an homage to Edith. "She's hidden in the background a lot, but she's been nothing but supportive and encouraging this entire time," Cynthia said. "The best way I can thank her is by putting her in a song because she's the one person that celebrated my music this entire time. I want her to hear that she's been celebrating me and that all the work she's put in has been noticed."

The support of her sister has also always meant so much to Cynthia. Three years younger than Cynthia, Stephanie was not drawn to the stage or screen. Her interest in sports sciences and health led to a career in preventive health care, the field of medicine that helps people avoid major diseases and injuries by enabling them to stop dangerous habits such as smoking or to improve nutrition to avoid diabetes. Stephanie encourages people to exercise to improve overall health. Cynthia shares Stephanie's dedication to sports and exercise as a form of health care.

Cynthia doesn't smoke or drink alcohol. She works out every day by running or going to a gym. Her Instagram account is filled with videos of her strenuous, imaginative workouts. The collection is called "Fitness."

"My body is muscular, and I won't shy away from it, which a lot of women are forced to do," Cynthia said. "I want to be able to do the Tom Cruise roles, the superhero roles."

Fame Gains

Cynthia lends her name, time, and resources to bring attention to causes she believes in. Organizations dedicated to equality, women's rights, diversity in the arts, and mental health are important to her. She has worked with organizations such as GLAAD (which campaigns for fair and accurate coverage of LGBTQ+ people in media), the NAACP (National Association for the Advancement of Colored People), and the Rush Philanthropic Arts Foundation. Rush provides art education to underserved young people.

Cynthia is an ambassador for the Power to the Patients campaign. An ambassador is a more formal word for a representative. The Power to the Patients campaign is working to raise awareness of a person's right to know the cost of medical services. "This is an incredibly important issue and I'm honored to join this campaign," Cynthia said. "A patient's right to access information regarding their health care is crucial and with this movement I hope we can engage and shed a light around this conversation."

CHAPTER 6
Broadway to Books

Cynthia entered the world of children's literature with the September 2021 publication of her first picture book, *Remember to Dream, Ebere*. The book is illustrated by Charnelle Pinkney Barlow. Cynthia wrote the story, which is about a young girl who dares to dream big with her mother's loving encouragement.

Cynthia returned to film in 2022, playing the Blue Fairy in the live-action version of *Pinocchio* from Disney. She joined Idris Elba on television in *Luther: The Fallen Sun*, a movie based on the detective Idris played in a popular crime drama on British television.

Cynthia's voice has earned her very special opportunities. On December 3, 2023, she sang for the second time in the Kennedy Center Opera House, this time to honor singer Dionne Warwick, one of the John F. Kennedy Center for the Performing Arts' honorees for lifetime artistic achievements. The Kennedy Center Honors ceremonies, first held in 1978, celebrate entertainers for their lifetime contributions to American culture through music, dance, theater, opera, movies, or television. The forty-sixth annual Kennedy Center honorees were actor Billy Crystal, opera singer Renée Fleming, singer and producer Barry Gibb, rapper and actress Queen Latifah, and singer Dionne Warwick.

Each honoree was treated to a special performance. Lin-Manuel Miranda, who created and wrote the songs for the musical *Hamilton* and the Disney movies *Moana* and *Encanto*, and actor Robert De Niro were two of those chosen to honor Billy Crystal. Rappers MC Lyte, Monie

Love, and D-Nice performed for Queen Latifah, who was also paid tribute by Missy Elliott. Opera stars Ailyn Pérez, Angel Blue, and Nadine Sierra serenaded Renée Fleming with a piece called "Song to the Moon." Singers Michael Bublé and Ben Platt each sang hit Bee Gees songs for Barry Gibb, who created the Bee Gees with his brothers Robin and Maurice.

Gladys Knight, known as the "Empress of Soul," and Chloe Bailey also sang for Dionne Warwick. When it was time for her to sing, Cynthia took to the stage in a striking sky-blue gown and with her head shaved. She sang "Alfie," one of Dionne Warwick's most famous songs. The audience began applauding before the song was over. Dionne Warwick smiled proudly the whole time Cynthia performed. Her hand on her heart after the performance, Cynthia bowed to Dionne Warwick and said, "I love you, Ms. Warwick."

Cynthia's first performance at the Kennedy Center Honors was in December 2016. It gave her another chance to meet her biggest hero, Aretha Franklin, who was a Kennedy Center Honoree in 1994.

They had met very briefly earlier in 2016, when Cynthia was on Broadway in *The Color Purple*. "We met her afterward, she came backstage, she sang the line 'I'm here' back to me, so I couldn't have been happier after that," Cynthia said.

She met Aretha again right before Cynthia's Kennedy Center Honors performance. "I saw her when I was about to perform and she remembered me and was like, 'Oh you, you can sing!'" Cynthia recalled, glowing with excitement. "I was like, 'I'm happy! That's it! I don't need anything else.'"

Aretha was in the audience when Cynthia performed "The Impossible Dream" in a tribute to John F. Kennedy. The audience, which included President Barack Obama and his wife, Michelle, gave Cynthia a standing ovation. Aretha's reaction to her singing touched Cynthia's heart. Aretha had listened to Cynthia with her eyes closed and wore a slight smile, swaying from side to side and singing along in obvious delight. Cynthia was humbled and amazed.

Aretha Franklin passed away in 2018. In 2021, when she portrayed Aretha in *Genius: Aretha*, Cynthia hoped Aretha knew that someone who truly admired her and loved her music was portraying her.

Cynthia's biggest project to date just might be the one that helps her collect the *O* in EGOT. She is portraying Elphaba, the young woman with green skin who became the Wicked Witch of the West in the Land of Oz, in the two-part movie version of the wildly popular musical

Wicked. The musical is based on the novel *Wicked* by Gregory Maguire. The film costars pop star and former Nickelodeon actor Ariana Grande as Glinda. *Wicked: Part One* is scheduled for release on November 27, 2024.

The roles are the biggest in the careers of both of these multitalented performers. Cynthia and Ariana grew as close as sisters during the long months of filming. They even have matching tattoos on their hands to commemorate their time working together. The tattoos are two simple words: "For Good."

"For Good" is one of the songs in *Wicked.* It's a duet in which Glinda and Elphaba, though destined to follow very different paths in life, sing about the positive impacts they've made on each other's lives.

Cynthia and Ariana are thrilled with their roles, but once again, there are critics who have complained about Cynthia's casting. They took to social media to question the casting of a Black woman as Elphaba, a green woman, while ignoring

the heart of the very words Elphaba herself sings: "Everyone deserves the chance to fly."

Cynthia and Ariana Grande

Whether critics like her in the role, and whether the role leads to an *O* to complete her EGOT, Cynthia has no doubt in her ability to honor the music, her costars, and audiences by giving them the very best Elphaba she possibly can. Just as she has in every other role she has taken on, Cynthia won't just fly. She will soar.

Timeline of Cynthia Erivo's Life

1987 — Cynthia Onyedinmanasu Chinasaokwu Erivo is born on January 8 in Stockwell, London, England

2010 — Graduates from the Royal Academy of Dramatic Art

2011 — Stars in United Kingdom touring musical of *Sister Act*

2013 — Stars as Celie Harris in off–West End production of *The Color Purple* musical

2015 — Reprises lead role as Celie Harris in Broadway revival of *The Color Purple* musical

2016 — Wins Tony Award for Best Performance by an Actress in a Leading Role in a Musical, *The Color Purple*

2017 — Wins Daytime Emmy Award for the cast of *The Color Purple*

— Wins Grammy Award for Best Musical Theater Album, *The Color Purple*

2018 — Stars in movie *Widows*

— Stars in movie *Bad Times at the El Royale*

2019 — Stars as abolitionist Harriet Tubman in the movie *Harriet*

2021 — Portrays Aretha Franklin in *Genius: Aretha*

— Releases debut solo album *Ch. 1, Vs. 1* in September

2022 — Plays the Blue Fairy in Disney's live-action movie *Pinocchio*

2024 — Plays Elphaba in the movie musical *Wicked: Part One*

Timeline of the World

1987 —	Aretha Franklin becomes the first woman inducted into the Rock and Roll Hall of Fame
1992 —	The Maastricht Treaty is signed, leading to the creation of the European Union
1998 —	Google is founded in Menlo Park, California
2006 —	The television show *Hannah Montana* debuts on the Disney Channel
2012 —	Britain's Queen Elizabeth II celebrates her Diamond Jubilee, the sixtieth anniversary of her coronation
2015 —	Justin Trudeau is sworn in as Canada's twenty-third prime minister
2018 —	*Avengers: Infinity War* is the year's highest-grossing movie
2019 —	Donald Trump becomes the third president in US history to be impeached
2020 —	The COVID-19 pandemic begins
2022 —	Russia invades Ukraine on February 24
2023 —	India surpasses China as the country with the most people: 1.4 billion

Bibliography

*Books for young readers

*Erivo, Cynthia. *Remember to Dream, Ebere*. Illustrated by
Charnelle Pinkney Barlow. New York: Little, Brown Books for
Young Readers, 2021.

Montgomery, Daniel. "Cynthia Erivo wins Daytime Emmy for
'The Color Purple,' is now just an Oscar away from EGOT."
Gold Derby, April 29, 2017. https://www.goldderby.com/
article/2017/cynthia-erivo-daytime-emmy-the-color-purple-
egot/.

Paulson, Michael. "The Actress Cynthia Erivo Rises With 'The Color
Purple.'" *New York Times*, December 22, 2015. https://www.
nytimes.com/2015/12/23/theater/the-actress-cynthia-erivo-
rises-with-the-color-purple.html.

Rose, Steve. "How Cynthia Erivo took the US by storm - with a little
help from Aretha and Oprah." *Guardian*, November 22, 2019.
https://www.theguardian.com/film/2019/nov/22/cynthia-
erivo-harriet-tubman-aretha-and-oprah.

Stafford, Zach. "Actress Cynthia Erivo Wants to Tell You a Story."
L'Officiel, February 14, 2023. https://www.lofficielusa.com/
film-tv/cynthia-erivo-luther-the-fallen-sun-wicked-movie-
cover-interview.